Crocodile Dog

Gene Kemp

D1134439

Illustrated by
ELIZABETH MANSON-BAHR

HEINEMANN · LONDON

William Heinemann Ltd
10 Upper Grosvenor Street, London W1X 9PA

LONDON · MELBOURNE
AUCKLAND · JOHANNESBURG

First published 1987
Text © 1987 Gene Kemp
Illustrations © 1987 Elizabeth Manson-Bahr

A school pack of BANANA BOOKS 19–24 is
available from Heinemann Educational Books
ISBN 0 435 00103 5

434 93043 1
Printed in Hong Kong by
Mandarin Offset

Chapter One

'IT DOESN'T LOOK like a nice dog,' I
said.

My sister Agg, known as The Agg,
came through the doorway with this
dog on a long piece of string. Then she
said at the top of her voice (and she's
got a voice like a fire engine siren,
dar-da, dar-da, you know what I mean),

'He's lost. So I brought him home
with me. He's a nice dog.'

I looked at it and it looked at me.

It was long, and low on the ground with short hairy legs, a coat like a coconut and a long, thin, ratty tail. Nearly worst of all were its little mean eyes, one brown, the other blue. But really worst of all was its great long snout-face full of teeth, hundreds of them – sharp, pointed teeth.

It lifted up its snout-face and snarled at me. I jumped back, being chicken by

nature. This dog would make anyone chicken.

'Don't be stupid,' shouted The Agg. 'You can see he's a nice dog.'

The Agg is the bossiest person I know. She's a walking laser beam, nine foot high and she's only ten. I think she'll grow up to be a giantess. Sometimes I've wondered if she's an alien from outer space dropped here by accident or through some Great Plan of the Universe.

She's got this big swinging plait she uses to knock me out. And she's the best footballer in the school. I ask you.

Once I asked my mother if she was adopted but she said, 'Of course not. Whatever made you think that? Mary's your very own sister. Mary's her real name.' But Dad calls her Agatha Gripper, so we all call her The Agg.

I'm Gregory, but they all call me The Splodge. I've got a patch over one eye to stop me squinting and whenever I try to take it off for a minute The Agg tells on me, mean pig.

But back to *that dog*. The Agg picked it up and cuddled it. She wants to be a lion tamer when she grows up. I mean when she grows old. She's up high enough, already. And I'll say that for her. She must have nerves of steel. She pushed her face right into that snouty face with all those teeth and sang to it,

'Diddums a lovely dog then, diddums, diddums, diddums . . .'

It was really yucky.

'See how miserable he is,' she
shouted at me. 'He's a stray. And he's
been ill-treated. You can always tell.'

'It would be hard to ill-treat that
dog. It would have your hand off if you
tried anything.'

'Look. See how neglected he is. He

needs love and attention.'

She seized my hand and pushed it against his dirty coat. I jumped back.

'Poor thing,' cried The Agg. 'He's starving.'

'That's no reason for it to eat me.'

I backed right up against the television, hands tucked behind me.

'I'm gonna ask Mum if I can keep him. Where is she?'

'Gone shopping. With Flossie.'

Flossie is our old fat spaniel, kind and comfortable and dead lazy. When she goes for a walk she sits down every three minutes.

'Mum won't let you keep it. And what about Flossie? And the cat? They won't want a crocodile – I mean a dog like *that* about the place. And it might kill the mice in the shed. And the tortoise.'

'Rubbish,' bawled The Agg. 'They'll love him.'

'Look,' I said desperately. 'It must belong to somebody and they're probably looking for it right now. Missing it. Even crying for it.'

It didn't seem likely. I thought the owner was probably emigrating to Australia. But I kept going.

'Suppose you take it back to where you found it? Then someone might come for it.'

She stuck out her lips at me like she does when she's mad.

'He's mine now,' she said through her teeth, while the crocodile growled through his, 'and no one is going to take him away from me.'

'I tell you this,' and I knew it was a wally thing to say even as I said it, 'if that dog stays I'm leaving.'

'Good. I'll pack your case for you,' said The Agg.

The crocodile dog stayed of course.

And she called it Laddie.

Chapter Two

DAD SAID HE thought the dog was the nastiest thing he'd ever laid eyes on and he'd seen a few in his time. Mum said we must put an ad. in the paper in the Lost and Found Column. Then the

owners would claim it. They must be missing it, she said.

'I shouldn't think so,' Dad said.

Mum put out a bowl of food for it as well as for Flossie, and Zebra the cat. It tried to eat the cat's food, got its nose scratched, wolfed down Flossie's and finally ate its own while the cat sulked.

'If we put it outside it might run back to its real home,' I said hopefully.

'Good idea,' Dad said.

'I think you're beastly and horrible, horrible and beastly,' howled The Agg.

'This is his real home. Can't you see he's been with people who haven't loved him?'

'I'm not surprised,' said Dad, opening the door, putting it out, and getting his foot bitten. Fortunately he was wearing leather boots. He didn't let The Agg open the door for an hour. She shouted dreadfully, though not loud enough to drown the howling going on outside in the garden.

Three people rang up to complain about the noise and both next door neighbours came to the kitchen door to ask if we'd gone mad and what we were going to do about the zoo at the front.

Suddenly the crocodile dog bounded in, quite unaware of the trouble it was causing. With a happy grin showing all its hundreds of teeth it made a beeline for The Agg and put its head on her lap. She crouched over it making little

whimpering noises. Flossie glared from the sofa and the cat sulked on top of the cupboard.

'I'll take it to the Police Station,' said Dad.

'The RSPCA would be better,' said Mum.

The Agg wailed. The dog snuggled closer to her.

'But it's a bit late,' Mum went on. 'It's probably closed by now.'

'Oh, it can stay tonight, then,' groaned Dad. 'As long as it's quiet. But only for tonight, mind.'

Chapter Three

I SUPPOSE I knew all along that it would stay. Whatever The Agg wants, The Agg gets. Mum put an ad. in the paper. No one came. Dad walked it all round the place where The Agg had first found it. No good. No one wanted to know.

One evening when she was at her music lesson, I bravely put on its lead, which The Agg had bought with her own money. I took it to the park and then I let it go and ran home, but it was no good. It got back before me.

'It used to be so peaceful before that dog came,' said Mum at breakfast one morning. She'd had to apologise to the next-door neighbour. Their cat had been stuck on the

roof all
night, chased there by Laddie.
It was still dark when the fire brigade
arrived to get it down.

'It's not his fault,' cried The Agg.
'Things annoy him.'

'I'll annoy him if he doesn't mend
his ways,' said Dad. 'He might just end
up in a Dogs' Home for Bad Animals.
Or even in a cat food tin.'

You should've heard The Agg. She

howled and cried and stamped her feet,
tears spouting everywhere like
fountains. So I went to school where it
seemed quite peaceful after home.

Mr Clark is our teacher. He's all
right, though he has got a temper. My
friends there are Pete, and Jackie
Brown, who's a girl but OK otherwise.
There's a big kid there with red hair
called Foxy Lewis and you have to look
out for him. He gets black moods and
then . . . TROUBLE!

The morning was fine. We did some
Maths. I wrote a story. We had Science
and I did some work on my Space

Project. After dinner we changed into our kit because it was football first of all. We picked teams and began to play. The sun was shining. For the first time ever I shot a goal. Then I shot another goal.

I felt absolutely brill. What a wonderful world.

'Dead lucky you are,' came Foxy Lewis's sneery voice right behind me. 'Or else you cheat.' He tried to trip me up but I whipped out of the way.

It was Foxy who fell in the mud.

'Stop messing about, Lewis,' cried Sir.

I felt even greater as we started up once more.

I ran down the pitch dribbling the ball and it was with me all the way until . . .

'What's that animal doing here? Get it off the pitch,' shouted Mr Clark.

I shot and missed. The whistle blew.

'Offside,' shouted Mr Clark. 'And

somebody get rid of that dog before it ruins the game.'

I turned from the goal. In the middle of the pitch a whirlpool raced at fantastic speed, a flying, barking, snapping whirlpool with a long thin ratty tail attached to it.

'Get out of here,' Sir was shouting, trying to send the whirlpool to the other side of the field. It swirled up and round and over him.

'Ouch, you beast. That was me,' Sir cried.

'It's a mad dog.'

'I'll get it for you, Sir.'

'Look out, it bites!'

'Look at all those teeth!'

'It's Splodge's dog!'

'No, it's not! It's my sister's.'

'I don't care whose dog it is. Just send it off!'

The game had stopped, everything in

chaos, as Laddie the crocodile dog whirled up and down, round and round, snapping at the ball and the players and the goal posts and Sir.

Sir was trying to get the dog collar to hold it, when suddenly he slipped in the mud and fell, banging his head on the goal post. He lay on the ground absolutely still.

There were screams and shouts.

It seemed like the end of the world.

'You've killed him,' said Foxy Lewis to me.

'Fetch an ambulance.'

'Is he dead?'

'Fetch the Head teacher.'

'Fetch Splodge's sister.'

Children bent over Mr Clark.

Somebody was crying.

'It's all your fault,' Foxy Lewis said

to me.

And in the middle of all this the crocodile dog still ran up and down, round and round, lifting its nose in the air and snapping its hundreds of teeth.

I turned to fetch The Agg. It seemed to me she was the only one who could sort this lot out. But as I did, a figure appeared on the field. Mrs Parker, the Head teacher.

'Just you all stand still,' she said.

So we did.

Then she snapped her fingers at Laddie, the crocodile dog, and it ran over, tail down, stomach on the ground and lay at her feet, looking up at her in exactly the same way it looks at The Agg.

All was silent.

She ran over to Mr Clark, but he was already getting up to his feet, wobbling a bit, though. I was very glad to see he wasn't dead.

'Jackie Brown, you go inside with Mr Clark,' she said. 'Then someone can tell me what's happened.'

'It's all Splodge's fault,' said Foxy Lewis.

'Oh, no, it isn't,' I answered, managing not to cry.

'Well, you tell me about it anyway,' said Mrs Parker.

Chapter Four

SOME TIME LATER we sat in the
classroom, silent and subdued. We'd
changed out of our football kit and Mrs
Parker had said a few words to us.

Mr Clark had gone home with
concussion. Freddy, the caretaker, had
arrived to put Laddie, the crocodile dog,
in a shed. He said he wasn't doing this
on his own, not with those teeth
looking at him, thank you very much.
So Mrs Parker sent for The Agg, who
helped him imprison Laddie.

Then The Agg and me, we had to go
to Mrs Parker's room where she told us
that on no account was that dog to
come to school, or enter the
playground. She didn't wish to see it
again, not ever. Even The Agg looked

small when we came out together.

'Don't you dare say it's all my fault,' she hissed.

I didn't. I turned, put my tongue out at her and ran straight into the nit nurse. Of course I got told off again.

In the classroom a new teacher had arrived. Wow! I'd never seen anything like her. She'd got orange skirts down to her boots, and floating orange hair down to her waist, gynormous orange specs. Next to her, on the desk, sat a huge orange hat. She looked like a commercial for Eat More Fruit.

'D'you think she changes to green or red?' whispered my friend Pete.

'Hello, children,' she sang out. 'My name's Miss Elphick and we're going to have a simply super fun time.'

The class cheered up. This was certainly a change from Mr Clark. He didn't wear orange specs or talk about super fun times. Behind me I could hear Foxy Lewis making up rhymes for Elphick, and they weren't very nice.

'Children,' she cried again and her voice bounced off the walls and pinged in my head. We all waited.

'I want you all to *really* stretch.'

She reached up on tip toes stretching

her arms wider and wider. It was
amazing how wide she made herself.

'I'm filling the room,' she cried.

'She'll burst,' whispered my friend,
Pete.

'Her or the walls,' said Foxy Lewis.

She sank down a bit then put a finger
to her orange lips.

'I want you all to imagine you're
tiny seeds!'

'Now stand beside your chairs and
bend down and curl up tight into a
teeny weeny ball.'

There was a loud crash and a cry
from Tony.

'I'm too big, Miss.'

'Of course you are, my dears,' pinged her voice hitting several notes at once. 'I should have realised what fine big children you all are. Silly me. Now we'll push all these tables and chairs back against the walls and then we shall be free to MOVE AND GROW.'

We did.

'You,' she cried, pointing to Jackie, 'can run round and sprinkle rain on the seeds, so they start to grow.'

Jackie ran round and sprinkled.

We grew. I banged my head growing into a nearby table.

'Now I'm the SUN,' called out Miss Elphick.

'But you're a lady, Miss!'

'Not that sort of son! Just grow, grow, GROW!'

While we grew, she put on a tape.

'Grow to the music,' she cried.

A jar of flowers fell onto Tony as he grew to the music higher than anyone else.

'I'm soaking wet,' he bellowed.

'Never mind, boy. Just grow and grow. Enter into the spirit of Nature.'

We did. Plants grew and leapt and jumped around the room.

'Let it all happen!' trilled Miss Elphick.

And it did.

The door shot open and into the room flew a long furry animal with teeth like a crocodile and a tail like a

rat. Round and round it flew among the growing plants. Laddie, the crocodile dog had arrived to join in the super fun time.

Then everything went completely mad. Crocodile Dog headed straight for Foxy Lewis, every tooth glittering with menace. Foxy Lewis screamed and so did the rest of the class. Miss Elphick snatched her orange hat and charged after Crocodile Dog flapping it furiously.

'Owch,' shouted Foxy, nipped by Laddie and flipped by Miss Elphick's hat.

Later they said I was running away as I headed for the door to get out, but honestly, I thought the only thing to do was to fetch The Agg from the classroom next door.

'No, you don't. I'm coming too,'

shouted Foxy, right behind me pursued
by the crocodile dog being chased by
Miss Elphick hitting him with her hat.

'He's getting me,' cried Foxy, just as
Foxy got me, grab, and I fell splat,
bang, crash . . . wallop.

Chapter Five

THE SCHOOL ORCHESTRA was
playing bongo drums in my head,
boom, boom, de da, boom, BOOM.

I opened my eyes on the wrecked
classroom. Oh, no. Mrs Parker had
once more arrived and everything,
including time, had stopped except for
the crocodile dog who lay quivering
with love at her feet, and Jackie who
was helping me to mine. As I stood up
I could see, hanging from Laddie's
teeth, a large piece of orange material.

Miss Elphick was wrapping round her
all that remained of her floaty skirt.

The school orchestra stopped playing
bongo drums in my head. Everything
was quiet. Then Mrs Parker spoke.

'Jackie, you're a sensible girl. Take
this animal to the caretaker and ask

him to tie him up even more securely this time until Gregory and Mary can take him home.'

She looked very coldly at me and at the crocodile dog who drooped its tail and ears in sorrow.

Jackie went up to it and tried to pull it out of the classroom, but it wouldn't budge. Suddenly it ran to *me*! And lay at *my* feet!

'You'd better take him, Gregory. Jackie can go with you. The rest of us will . . . tidy up.'

Chapter Six

WE HURRIED OUT of the classroom at
speed. Jackie and me. I clutched the
Crocodile Dog's piece of string but
stayed as far away from it as possible.

None of it was fair. I hadn't done
anything. I didn't want the dog in the
first place. I didn't even like it. I hadn't
brought it to school. I couldn't help it if
Mr Clark got splatted and Miss Elphick
was orange and nutty. I liked Mr Clark
and I'd rather have had football
anytime. Somewhere, something wasn't
fair.

It was that rotten animal's fault.

I looked down at it and it looked up
at me, wagging its ratty tail.

'Come on, you,' I snapped, pulling
the string tightly (so that it hurt I
hoped).

But it didn't come. Crocodile Dog had stopped and wouldn't move. Wouldn't budge.

Tug, tug, tug. But it lay low on its belly, back legs braced, ears a-prick, eyes shining bright, every tooth a-gleam, low rumbling growls coming from its throat.

'What's up?' asked Jackie.

'Nothing. It's just being stupid, that's all.'

'Grrrr! Grrrh! Woof, woof, woof! Grrrh!'

'Oh, come on!'

It was no use. Crocodile Dog wouldn't go any further.

'What's got into you, you stupid animal?'

But Jackie had stopped dead too.

'Look! Look!' she cried, pointing at the cupboard beside us. Smoke was

curling round the edges of the doors.
Grey, wispy smoke. Very peculiar. I
went to look at what was wrong.

'No, no, don't! Don't, Splodge!'
shouted Jackie. 'Don't open those
doors! The cupboard's on fire!'

Too late. Grabbing a handle, I had
pulled the door open.

A lion's roar, a sheet of flame, a
rumbling and a thundering, a fierce
heat and a horrible scorching smell.

Jackie was shouting, 'Help, help.
Ring the fire alarm!'

A huge fat cloud of smoke billowed

all around us. My eyes streamed and I
started to splutter and cough, throat
burning. Jackie was screaming now.

'Fire! Fire! Help!'

Through the smoke loomed our
caretaker, Freddy, then the buzzer
sounded loud and terrifying, bells rang
and there was the noise of running feet
and people shouting. Then a voice
sounding clear and calm.

'Walk steadily, children. Keep in
line. Out of school into the playground.
Steadily, there. Everything's all right.'

And all the school was trooped safely away from the smoke and the heat and the flames.

I was safe too. For the crocodile dog had seized me with its hundreds of teeth and dragged me to safety, ready to be lined up and checked from the registers, out there on the playground, clear away from the danger with all the other children.

Much later we sat in Mrs Parker's office, The Agg, Jackie, Crocodile Dog and me. I had one bandaged hand which hurt dreadfully and he was licking the other one.

'I'm just writing a note to your parents,' explained Mrs Parker, 'to let them know what happened. And to say what a brave dog you've got there. A hero. With a bit more training he'll

grow up into a very nice dog.'

'Yes, I know,' said The Agg. 'I always knew he was a nice dog.'

She and Mrs Parker smiled as if they understood one another perfectly. The mad idea came into my head that The Agg would end up just like her one day. But I didn't care. I put out my hand, very cautiously – because I did ache an awful lot – and stroked Laddie's head. For a moment I was afraid he was going to bite it but no, he just went on licking instead.